# Little Squirts

by Debra Mostow Zakarin
Illustrated by Yakovetic

Grolier Books

Published by Grolier Books
© 1997 Disney Enterprises, Inc. No portion of
this book may be reproduced without the written
consent of Disney Enterprises, Inc.

Based on the book by Dodie Smith, published by
Viking Press

Produced by Bumpy Slide Books

Printed in the United States of America

ISBN: 0-7172-8790-4

Pongo and Perdita's puppies loved the Dalmatian Plantation. There was plenty of room to roam and play. Their parents were always taking them for nice, long walks. And Nanny's meals seemed even more delicious than the meals she had served in the city. Best of all, each day seemed to bring some new adventure.

Today was no different.

"Gather around!" Perdita called. "We have a surprise for you. Our pets, Roger and Anita, are taking us to town this afternoon."

"To town!" the pups exclaimed. "Hooray, we're going to town!"

"Now, now," Pongo said. "You must all be very good."

"Uh-oh," Patch loudly whispered to Lucky. "We gotta behave."

"You *have* to behave," corrected Perdita.

"We're all going to the town hall for a very important ceremony being held for my pet, Roger," Pongo said with pride.

"What kind of ceremony?" asked Dash.

"It's a surprise," answered Perdita.

"Will lunch be served at this very important ceremony?" asked Rolly.

"I don't think so, dear," Perdita said as she licked him on top of his head.

All the way to the town hall, Pongo and Perdita's black spotted pups tried hard to behave.

"Hey, Lucky! Stop poking me with your wet nose," complained Patch.

"It wasn't me," said Lucky. "It was Penny."

They padded along, passing the market, the firehouse, and the elementary school.

"I want to go to school," said Patch. "It looks like so much fun."

"The only school you'll ever go to is obedience school," teased Penny as they reached the town square.

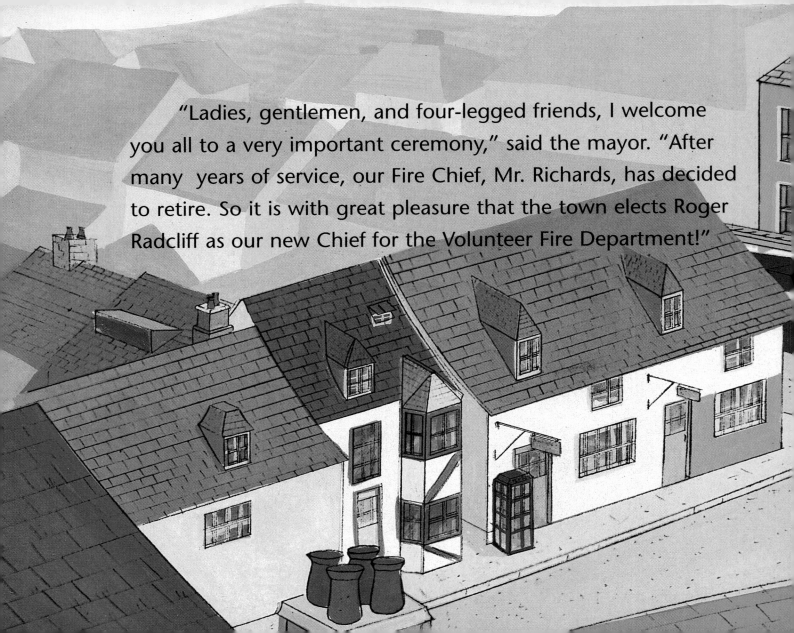

"Ladies, gentlemen, and four-legged friends, I welcome you all to a very important ceremony," said the mayor. "After many years of service, our Fire Chief, Mr. Richards, has decided to retire. So it is with great pleasure that the town elects Roger Radcliff as our new Chief for the Volunteer Fire Department!"

The puppies barked and wagged their tails. The townspeople clapped their hands.

"Oh, Roger," said Anita. "I'm so proud of you."

"Thank you, dear," replied Roger, blushing.

"But dear, what about your music?" asked Anita.

"Don't worry, darling," Roger replied. "Fires don't happen every day. I'll have plenty of time to write my songs."

"Won't Pongo miss you?" asked Anita.

"Of course not," Roger insisted. "Pongo will be there with me." He bent down and scratched behind the Dalmatian's ears. "Pongo, my boy, as Fire Chief of this town, I hereby appoint you as my Deputy Fire Dog."

It was Roger's and Pongo's first day to report for duty, and the pups couldn't have been more excited.

"Please, Father, please!" begged the pups. "Please can't we go to work with you and Roger?"

"I think that would be up to the Fire Chief," answered Pongo.

Not wasting a moment, the pups ran over to Roger and sat expectantly at his feet.

"Roger, I think the puppies want to go with you and Pongo," Nanny said, smiling.

"All right," Roger replied, patting a few of the pups on the head. "But no fooling around! Fighting fires is serious business!"

The first week at the firehouse, the other firefighters gave Roger and Pongo a tour of the firehouse. Then they showed the new Chief all of the equipment on the fire engine.

Next they demonstrated exactly what to do in case of a fire.
The puppies stayed on the sidelines, paying attention to
everything the men and women did.

"Sound the alarm, change into uniforms, load the fire engine, go to the fire, unroll the hoses, and spray the fire with water," said Roger, sitting down in his chair. "I don't know why firehouses have so many drills. Fighting fires is simple. We're ready to handle anything, don't you think?"

"Ruff, ruff!" Pongo barked proudly.

A week went by without a fire, and things were pretty
quiet at the firehouse. Then, one day, things got even quieter.
Every last firefighter was home in bed with the flu. As Roger
sat composing music, the phone rang. When he hung up, he
had butterflies in his stomach.

"Pongo, boy!" shouted Roger. "There's a fire at the town hall!"

Pongo was alarmed. Their first fire and they would have to fight it alone!

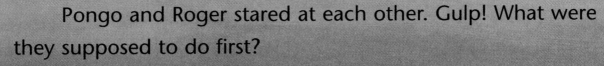

Pongo and Roger stared at each other. Gulp! What were they supposed to do first?

The puppies knew. They had been paying attention during the drills. They ran from one piece of equipment to another,

barking to let Roger know what to load onto the fire engine.
When it was ready, Pongo and the pups climbed aboard.
Roger struggled to get into his firefighting gear as fast as he
could. There was no time to lose!

Roger sounded the siren as he quickly drove to the town hall.

When they arrived, he saw smoke coming out of a ground-floor window. Roger unrolled the hose, attached it to the fire hydrant, and turned on the water. Roger and Pongo rushed inside while the pups kept the gathering crowd a safe distance away.

Roger and Pongo came out of the town hall a few
minutes later.

"Father, is everything okay?" asked the very worried pups.

"Yes. Luckily, it was only a small fire in the wastebasket.

Somebody was very careless with a match," Pongo explained. "And I'm so proud of you! You did the right thing by keeping everyone away. That way Roger and I were able to put out the fire and no one got hurt."

Just then Roger whistled for Pongo and the pups. He was standing on the sidewalk talking to the mayor himself.

"Well, little ones," the mayor said. "Roger tells me that if it weren't for all of your quick thinking and bravery, this fire could have really got out of hand. Therefore I'd like to officially declare you all honorary members of the Volunteer Fire Department!"

The next day, the pups, Pongo, and Roger reported to the firehouse for duty.

Roger turned to Pongo and said, "It seems there's more to being a Fire Chief than I thought. So today I'm going to inspect the equipment, read the safety manual, and go through a fire drill. Soon I may even know as much about this firehouse as our own little squirts!"

Pongo proudly looked at his pups. He hoped there wouldn't be any emergencies for at least an hour or so.

After all, even brave Deputy Fire Puppies need their naps.